Dunc and Amos
Meet the
Slasher

OTHER YEARLING BOOKS YOU WILL ENJOY:

THE HAYMEADOW, *Gary Paulsen*
THE COOKCAMP, *Gary Paulsen*
THE VOYAGE OF THE *FROG, Gary Paulsen*
THE BOY WHO OWNED THE SCHOOL, *Gary Paulsen*
THE RIVER, *Gary Paulsen*
THE MONUMENT, *Gary Paulsen*
HOW TO EAT FRIED WORMS, *Thomas Rockwell*
HOW TO FIGHT A GIRL, *Thomas Rockwell*
CHOCOLATE FEVER, *Robert Kimmel Smith*
BOBBY BASEBALL, *Robert Kimmel Smith*

YEARLING BOOKS/YOUNG YEARLINGS/YEARLING CLASSICS are designed especially to entertain and enlighten young people. Patricia Reilly Giff, consultant to this series, received her bachelor's degree from Marymount College and a master's degree in history from St. John's University. She holds a Professional Diploma in Reading and a Doctorate of Humane Letters from Hofstra University. She was a teacher and reading consultant for many years, and is the author of numerous books for young readers.

For a complete listing of all Yearling titles,
write to Dell Readers Service,
P.O. Box 1045, South Holland, IL 60473.

Gary Paulsen

Dunc and Amos Meet the Slasher

A YEARLING BOOK

Dunc and Amos Meet the Slasher

Chapter · 1

Duncan—Dunc—Culpepper was marking the floor in Amos's hallway with pieces of white tape.

"That was your best run yet. You went three feet, four and three quarter inches farther than the last time," Dunc said.

They had put together a ramp on the staircase with some plywood they found in the garage. Amos was riding his dad's leather office chair, the new one with six wheels, down the ramp and out to the hall.

Dunc was conducting an experiment on forward momentum. And he also had this thing about breaking records. He timed

each of the runs and marked the exact stopping point with a piece of tape.

Amos was at the top of the stairs. He pushed off with one foot and started rolling. He picked up speed. Everything around him was a complete blur.

Then the phone rang.

Amos's ears shot out like radar.

If Amos was within a two-mile radius of a ringing phone, he would try to answer it. He knew it was Melissa Hansen trying to call him.

Amos worshiped Melissa. He would have given anything if she would notice him. She never did. He was invisible to her. Once at school she hung her windbreaker on his ear, thinking he was the coat rack.

Dunc knew about Amos's problem with phones. He jumped out of the way just in time.

Amos came barreling down the ramp headed for the hall phone. His brain calculated the hall phone to be exactly seven point three centimeters from his fingertips. He made a try for the phone with his left hand.

He missed.

The chair came up on two wheels. It wobbled and came back down. He still might have been okay.

Except for the dog.

Scruff, his dog, chose that exact moment to run in from the living room. The chair hit the dog and tipped forward. It was like launching a missile.

Amos hit the front door headfirst.

When Dunc got to him, pieces of the door were everywhere. Amos's head and shoulders had gone completely through. Scruff was growling and gnawing on one of Amos's legs.

Dunc swung the door open so he could talk to him. "I got the phone for you. Your parents are going to be late. Someone stole their car stereo. They're at the police station. Your mom wants you to start dinner."

Amos was trying to shake the dog off of his leg and work his way out the door. He looked up at Dunc. "Unless you're busy—or doing something else—*get me out of here.*"

Dunc grabbed him by his feet and pulled.

3

Amos fell out on the floor. He was a mass of splinters.

Scruff took one last bite out of his leg and jumped outside through the hole in the door.

Amos's shirt was shredded and one pant leg was mangled. Dunc could see the neighbors across the street through the hole in the door.

Amos tried to focus. He looked at the hole in the door. "They sure don't make doors like they used to," he said.

"I hope your dad sees it that way," Dunc said.

"We've been needing a new door anyway. That one is at least two years old. Hey, did you see that slick move I made when I got near the phone? I almost did it this time. An Olympic downhill skier probably wouldn't have had much better style. Did you see how I corrected my form at the last minute?"

Dunc nodded.

"Who did you say was on the phone?"

"Your parents. They want you to start dinner."

4

"Oh. I already did."

"I don't smell anything."

"That's because it's a cold dinner. You don't have to cook sauerkraut and ketchup sandwiches."

Dunc turned green.

"By the way," Amos said, "can I eat over at your house tonight?"

Chapter · 2

Dunc was sitting at his computer deep in thought. Amos was bouncing a softball off the bedroom wall. "What are you thinking about?"

"I was wondering if the police will be able to catch the guys that stole your car stereo," Dunc said.

"They told my parents it could take a while. There's been a whole string of these burglaries in the last month. So far they don't have any leads."

"Hmmm."

"Don't start that."

"What?"

"Whenever you make that sound, it always means trouble for me. Remember when I was stuck in that chimney? It all started with that dumb sound."

Dunc shrugged. "I thought since it was your car, you might want to help find out who did it."

"My dad says his insurance will cover it. I'm not worried. Besides, school starts tomorrow and I've got more important things to worry about."

"Like what?"

"Like making sure Melissa has the desk next to mine in homeroom."

Dunc turned off the computer. Amos Binder was his lifetime best friend. He knew if he let him get started talking about Melissa, he would talk all night.

"Let's go to the mall and see how everybody is spending their last night of freedom," Dunc said.

Amos jumped up. "Good idea. Maybe we'll run into Melissa."

The Pioneer Mall was only a fifteen-minute bike ride from Dunc's house. They took

the shortcut through the abandoned housing development.

They coasted into the parking lot of the mall. Red lights were flashing everywhere. Two police cars were parked behind a new yellow Mustang.

Dunc stopped his bike a few feet away. An officer was taking a statement from the woman who owned the car.

"I was only in the mall for a few minutes. My car was definitely locked. When I got back, my stereo was gone." The woman stared at the hole in her dashboard.

The officers checked around for witnesses, but no one had seen anything.

Amos was in a hurry to get to the video games. He tapped Dunc's shoulder. "Come on. We don't have much time."

Dunc held up his hand. "Wait a minute. I want to see what happens."

Before the police officer left, he assured the woman that everything possible would be done to find her stereo.

Dunc walked his bike up closer. "Excuse me, ma'am. My friend here just had his

stereo stolen too. Would it be okay if we looked around? The police might have missed something."

The woman nodded her head. "You might as well. I don't see how it could hurt."

Amos held Dunc's bike while he looked around by the car. He searched like a bloodhound, but nothing seemed out of place. He was about to leave when he looked through the front window. Something shiny caught his eye. He opened the door, reached in, and picked up a silver bead.

"Does this belong to you?" Dunc asked.

She took it out of his hand. "I don't recognize it. It might belong to my daughter. I'm not sure."

"Do you mind if I keep it?"

The woman shook her head. "I don't know what good it will do. But sure. Go ahead."

Dunc put the bead in his pocket. "Come on, Amos. We better get going."

Chapter · 3

There were kids all over the mall. It was an every-year, last-night-before-school ritual. Everybody came to the mall to discuss teachers, classes, clothes, and strategy.

Amos kept an eye out for Melissa while they played Galaxy Snot-Ranger at the video arcade.

"Don't you think it's kind of interesting that these car burglars only hit cars at the mall?" Dunc asked.

"Where would you go if you needed about a thousand empty cars?"

"It's okay, I guess, but you'd think they'd

11

move around. To make sure nobody caught on."

Amos shrugged. "They seem to be doing just fine without your help. Give me another quarter. I'm up to two hundred thousand points. I'm about to max out and break the all-time snot record."

A group of girls walked past the entrance of the arcade.

Amos quit punching buttons and sort of floated over to the door. Melissa was one of the girls.

"Amos, what about your game?"

"You finish it for me. Mr. Smooth is now on the job."

Oh, great, Dunc thought.

Amos hurried past the girls. He positioned himself at the end of the mall by the water fountain, leaned casually up against the wall, and waited.

Melissa and her friends were walking toward the fountain. It looked like it might actually work.

Except that the wall Amos was leaning on was a door. The door to the women's rest room. An elderly lady with a cane pulled the

door open from the inside. Amos had all his weight on his elbow. He lost his balance and fell sideways into the rest room.

Dunc couldn't see him anymore. But it didn't matter. Amos could be located by all the screaming and yelling from the rest room.

The lady started beating him with her cane. "You pervert! This will teach you to mess with a defenseless woman."

Amos tried crawling away from the woman, but she hit him harder and kicked him in the ribs for good measure. It started a chain reaction. Another woman joined in with her umbrella. One lady got in a couple of licks with her purse. Then she pulled out a can of Mace.

When Amos finally got away, he was beaten to a pulp. He walked like a mass of quivering Jell-O.

Melissa and her friends had disappeared.

Dunc helped him walk back out to the bicycle rack. "Are you okay?"

Amos looked up at him with his one good eye. The other one was swollen shut. "Never felt better."

"I don't think Mr. Smooth impressed Melissa."

"Why don't you rub a little salt on my cut lip while you're at it?"

Dunc shrugged. "I was just telling you so you wouldn't try this particular move next time."

Amos tried to throw his leg up over his bike. "There won't be a next time. She probably thinks I'm a complete geek and will never call me or even speak to me again."

"She doesn't speak to you now." Dunc sighed. "Besides, there's a chance she didn't know it was you."

Amos's face brightened a little. "You think maybe?"

"I think you fell in the door before she could be sure who it was."

Amos smiled. "I can live with that. If we hurry, we might be able to catch up with her."

He pedaled off toward Melissa's house.

Dunc sighed. "Maybe I should have told him the truth."

Chapter · 4

The first day of school. It had an exciting yet deadly ring to it.

Dunc was up two hours early arranging the contents of his notebook and backpack in alphabetical order. Even his pens and pencils were in perfect alignment. All pens were placed lettering-side-up, and every pencil was exactly the same length.

Amos was tending to business also.

He was in his dad's bathroom splashing the "green stuff" on his face. He slapped it on until his cheeks were sore. Then he poured it on his hair and rubbed it in.

When they met in front of Amos's house,

Dunc wished he had brought a gas mask. Amos had a smell that traveled thirty feet in front of him.

Dunc held his nose. "That stuff should be illegal. You should be arrested for polluting the environment."

Amos sniffed in the air. "I don't smell anything. Besides, the label says a little of this stuff will drive a girl wild."

"I can certainly understand that. The fumes are toxic."

Dunc made him ride on the opposite side of the road all the way to school.

The schoolyard was alive with music and conversation. Dunc and Amos locked their bikes in the rack just as the first bell rang.

Their first class was homeroom with Miss Monroe.

Miss Monroe was new this year. She was blond, pretty, and very inexperienced. She said they could sit anywhere they wanted.

Freddie—the Zit—Pittman took her up on it. He sat in her chair.

The class was pretty much in chaos. Paper planes were flying everywhere, and a

couple of the kids in the back were using a work table for break dancing.

Dunc was reading a copy of *Computer Weekly*. Amos had managed to get the chair behind Melissa's. He was hanging on every word she said to her second-best friend Steffie Thompson—until Melissa took a deep breath, held her nose, and moved to another desk.

Everything came to a complete standstill when the door opened and the principal walked in. Not because of the principal but because of the student with her.

He was no run-of-the-mill, ordinary kid. He had outrageous red spiky hair and an earring in one ear. He was older and outweighed everybody in class by fifty pounds. His clothes were black. All black. Including a leather jacket with zippers and metal stuff all over it.

The principal handed Miss Monroe some paperwork and left.

"Class, I want you to meet . . . Slasher Davis. Unusual name. Just have a seat anywhere."

Slasher's eyes narrowed as he looked

17

around the room. Finally they fixed on a desk in the back.

It was Amos's desk.

Slasher swaggered to the back of the room. He picked up the desk and dumped Amos out on the floor.

"Thanks, Teach. I'll take this one."

Amos pulled his face up off the floor and sat up. "Nice to meet you, Slasher. Hope you like the desk."

The bell rang.

There was a mad dash for the door. Slasher deliberately stepped on Amos's hand as he left.

Dunc helped him up. "What a creep. Do you need to go to the nurse or anything?"

"No, I'm okay. That guy is just lucky I'm in a good mood. Otherwise there might have been bloodshed."

"Yeah, yours."

Amos picked up his books. "You forget those kung fu classes I took. I'm a deadly weapon."

"Amos, you only took two classes."

"What are you saying?"

"Maybe you should just try to stay out of his way."

"Okay, but it's not because I'm afraid or anything. It's only because you want me to."

"Thank you, Amos." Dunc smiled and grabbed his books.

The morning classes went a little better than homeroom. Except for PE, when Amos got his head a little too close to the bow in archery, and part of his eyebrows ended up stuck to the target.

At lunch they sat at their regular table. Tommy Farrel and Jesse Perez were involved in a burping contest. Tommy had just let one go that shook the building.

What happened next shouldn't have. It was just one of those unlucky turn of events.

Amos got up to return his tray. His foot caught the edge of the table. He did a full somersault and came up on his feet. It was amazing. The only problem was that he lost the tray.

It flew to the next table and landed in a kid's lap. But not just any kid.

Slasher Davis.

Mashed potatoes stuck out in little clumps on his spiked hair. He was not a happy camper.

Before Slasher was through, Amos was wearing the tray around his neck. An orange was stuck on his nose, and two milk cartons were attached to his ears.

Dunc helped him get the tray off before he choked to death. "I told you to stay away from that guy."

Amos looked at him.

A cafeteria worker walked over and chewed Amos out for damaging school property. She told him he'd have to pay for the tray.

The bell rang.

Chapter·5

School was over for the day. They were sitting on the bed in Amos's room. Or Amos was sitting. Dunc was afraid to sit on the bed. Amos had a lifetime collection of trash, food, and clothes under that bed. Dunc preferred to stand. That way he could see if anything crawled out.

"As I see it, we have two big problems," Dunc said. "The stereo thieves and Slasher Davis."

"I no longer have either of those problems." Amos put his hands behind his head and leaned back. "My dad just got a new

stereo, and I am never going back to school."

"You have to go school. It's a law."

"I read somewhere, when your life is in danger, that law is null and void."

Dunc started straightening the desk. "Your life isn't in danger. Slasher just told you to stay out of his face."

"And I intend to. I may move to Canada."

"You're taking the wrong attitude with this thing. I have a plan—"

"Hold it right there. Your plans are bad. Worse than bad. They're defective, demented, and harmful to my body."

"This one isn't." Dunc moved to the dresser. He straightened it.

Amos waited.

He moved to the closet and began to color code Amos's shirts.

"Stop that!" Amos yelled. "Are you going to tell me or what?"

Dunc went back to the desk and started sharpening pencils.

"If you don't stop that, I'm going to shove those pencils up your nose. I like my room

just the way it is. It has character. Now—are you going to tell me?"

"No, you're probably right. We probably couldn't pull it off. It might not be worth it to try to make Slasher your friend anyway."

"My friend?" Amos swung his legs around so he could face Dunc.

"Yeah, have you seen that strange group he hangs out with? I noticed they're all sort of like him."

Amos hugged his knees. "You mean big, ugly, and illiterate?"

"In a way. But they all dress the part. That's the key. I was thinking we could dress you up like one of his gang. Maybe then he'd leave you alone."

"I don't know. I have my image to think of."

"Right."

"Okay—so I don't have an image. But I'm still not so sure about this. Where would we get the clothes?"

Dunc smiled. "Your sister, Amy."

"You can't be serious. I wouldn't be caught dead in her clothes. Which, by the

way, is exactly what I would be if she found out. So forget it."

Dunc threw up his hands. "Okay. If you want to be on the run for the rest of the school year . . ."

Amos thought for a moment. "I don't get it. How would wearing a girl's clothes help me?"

"Not just any girl's. Amy's. Remember when she went through that motorcycle phase? She had a black leather jacket and a boyfriend named Eagle."

Amos grinned. "It was Vulture. He used to park his motorcycle in our living room and rev the engine. I'm pretty sure my dad paid him to leave town. Amy got over him though. She's into granola clothes now."

"Perfect." Dunc headed for the door. "She won't be needing her jacket and stuff."

"Stop!"

"What's the matter now?"

"You forget. Amy said she'd dismember me, among other terrible things, if I ever went near her room. I believe her."

"No problem. You stand at the door and keep watch. I'll look for the stuff."

Dunc found a cardboard box in the back of Amy's closet. It had everything they needed. It also contained her personal diary for the last five years.

Amos was excited. Not about the clothes. About the diary.

"Do you know what this means?" Amos asked.

Dunc shook his head.

"This"—Amos waved the diary—"means I won't have to wash dishes for years."

"People really shouldn't read other people's personal stuff," Dunc said.

Amos laughed. "This from a person who just broke into another person's room. Don't try to talk me out of it. You don't have to live with her. I need some kind of leverage."

Dunc shrugged. "Well, come on then. We don't have much time. Mr. Johnson gave us homework, remember?"

Chapter · 6

"Amos, you look great. Quit worrying."

They were on their way to the cafeteria. So far, Slasher hadn't shown up at school. Amos hoped he was taking a permanent holiday.

Amos scratched under the sweaty leather jacket. "I've been giving this thing some thought. I'm not sure I want to be friends with a guy who stomps people into the ground."

"Who told you he does that?" Dunc asked.

"Tommy Farrel got it straight from Eddy Sanders, who got it from Joey Bates, who

personally knows a guy who's seen him do it."

"Amos, you can't believe everything you hear."

"That's not all. I've also heard that he carries a switchblade knife and once in a fight, he cut off some guy's fingers. Now he wears them on a chain around his neck."

"Don't be silly. If he'd done all that, he'd be in a reformatory or something."

"Well, I'm not taking any chances. I'm getting out of this before it's too late."

Amos felt a grip on his shoulder. "Hey, you—dorkhead. What do you think you're doing? Are you making fun of me?"

He turned around.

Slasher.

Amos gulped. "I was just—"

Dunc interrupted. "Haven't you heard that imitation is the sincerest form of flattery? My friend here wants to join your gang."

Slasher closed one eye and thought about it. He turned to Amos. "You and the Brain take a seat in here." He shoved them through the cafeteria doors in front of him.

As he walked away, something fell off of Slasher's jacket and rolled under the table. Dunc reached down and picked it up.

A shiny silver bead.

Dunc stuffed it into his pocket.

Slasher and his gang had taken over the far corner of the cafeteria. Amos and Dunc could see him from across the room talking and pointing toward them. In a few minutes whatever they were talking about was settled and he started walking back their way.

"Dunc, I really don't think this is a good idea."

"We'll be fine. This may be just the break we need. Trust me."

"You always say that. Things never work out when you say that."

"Quit worrying. Underneath, they're probably regular guys like everybody else."

Slasher moved to Amos. "The brotherhood says you can come."

Dunc got up to follow.

Slasher put his hand on Dunc's chest. "Not you, Brain."

Amos had the look of a trapped rabbit. He glanced over his shoulder at Dunc.

29

Dunc motioned for him to go on.

Amos decided to be cool or die trying. He moved his hands up and down as if he were pushing air. He shuffled his feet.

When they got to the corner of the cafeteria, he was really into the part. He bobbed his head up and down. "I'm bad. I'm mean. I'm—"

Amos stepped on his shoestring and did a flip over the table, cracking his head on the floor. Finally his vision cleared and he stood up.

". . . tough. I'm cool."

"How'd you do that, man?" A short kid with his name shaved into one side of his hair stepped over to him.

Amos swallowed hard. "That? That was nothing. I do stuff like that all the time."

The kid put his thumb in the air. "I pronounce this dude awesome."

Slasher pounded him on the back. "See, I told you guys he'd do. What's your name, man?"

Amos bit his lip. "Name?"

"Yeah, you know." He pointed at some of

the gang. "This here is Hammer, Crusher, Spit, and Claw."

Amos tried to think. In the toughest voice he could manage, he said, "Dirt Bag. My name is Dirt Bag. Dirt for short."

Chapter · 7

"Dirt Bag? Couldn't you have done better than Dirt Bag?" Dunc asked.

Amos shrugged. "I was on the spot. It's what Amy calls me, and it just popped into my head. But that's not why I called you over here."

"I know why you called me. Today is Saturday. Your dad said we better have that plywood stacked neatly in the garage by Saturday or else."

Amos pointed at his desk. "Wrong. Take a look at that stack of books over there."

"I don't see any books."

Amos moved a broken model, a half-

eaten pepperoni pizza, a T-shirt, and a pair of jeans. "Now look."

"Okay. You have a stack of books on your desk. Am I supposed to be impressed?"

"That stack of books is why I called you over here. I need to discuss one tiny little flaw in your big plan for me to be friends with Slasher."

Dunc sat on the edge of the dresser. "I don't understand. I thought everything was going great between you two."

"Oh, everything is just fine—as long as I have his homework ready for him on Monday."

"Are you serious?"

Amos nodded his head. "As a heart attack. He also wants me to carry his books to and from school, polish his bike, and get his lunch, and do anything else his twisted mind can come up with."

"Amos, you can't do someone else's homework. It's not ethical."

Amos stared at him for a few minutes. "That's it? That's all you're going to say? No . . . 'I'm sorry,' or, 'My plan was really stupid' . . . or anything?"

"At this point, I don't think my saying I'm sorry would help your situation."

"No. But it might help yours. Because if you don't say it—"

Dunc held up his hand. "Okay. If it makes you happy, I am willing to acknowledge that my stratagem did not incorporate an emergency contingency for this specific development."

Amos looked at him suspiciously. "Is that the same as saying you messed up?"

"In a way."

"Good. Now, how are we going to get me out of this?"

Dunc started to pace the floor. He thought out loud. "Well, you obviously can't be this guy's personal slave. We'll just have to handle it another way."

"I still think Canada is the best idea. Or better yet—the North Pole. He'd never find me at the North Pole. I could blend in with the elves."

Dunc stopped. "Maybe if we talked to the principal or one of the counselors?"

Amos got his suitcase out of his closet. "If

I left right now, I could probably be there in a couple of months."

"Of course, talking to the principal could make matters worse. Slasher might try to get back at you some way," Dunc said.

Amos was throwing everything he owned into the suitcase. "I wonder if my bike is in good enough shape to make it through all that ice and snow."

Dunc moved over to Amos. "Maybe you could explain to Slasher that you don't do other people's homework because you have a hard enough time doing your own."

Amos snapped his fingers. "I know— Amy! Amy would be glad to buy me a one-way ticket to the North Pole."

"Amos, you're not going to the North Pole."

"Why not? Have you thought of a better hiding place?"

"You're not going anywhere. I'm going to figure a logical way out of this."

"That's what I'm afraid of."

Chapter · 8

Amos pedaled his bike up even with Dunc's. "Tell me again why we're doing this."

"Because it never hurts to have the upper hand. If we're going to solve your problem, we need some inside information. If we can find out how Slasher thinks, we'll be that much farther ahead."

"Slasher doesn't think. He operates solely on killer instinct. Which is why we shouldn't be spying on him."

"Look, Amos, you knowing the location of the gang's hangout is a real stroke of luck. It might be just the break we need. Besides,

I've got a hunch about what we might find. I wonder why they told you."

"They didn't exactly tell me. I sort of overheard them talking about it when I was getting Slasher's chocolate milk. He still owes me for the milk."

Dunc coasted down a little hill and then pulled over to the side of the road. Amos followed him.

"Let's go over it again."

Amos made a face. "You always make me go over things. Do you think I'm brainless? It's not that hard."

"Humor me, okay?"

Amos groaned. "If the gang is inside, we sneak up and try to listen. If they're not, you'll go in and look around while I keep watch."

"Good. We should be at the waterfront in a few minutes. Be careful and stay close." Dunc pushed off.

"Wait!" Amos yelled. "I need to talk to you about this waterfront thing. Last time we were down there, we barely made it out in one piece. People who value their lives don't go down there in broad daylight."

He was talking to air. Dunc was already out of sight.

Amos kicked the dirt. "Maybe I just won't go with him this time. Maybe I'll turn around right here. I'll head north and keep on going."

He sat on his bike for a full five seconds. Then he followed.

Dunc was waiting for him on the outskirts of the waterfront. "I've spotted the old grocery store. The gang's not there. The only problem is the two guys across the street from the store."

Amos swallowed. "Two guys—you mean waterfront types—guys who drink out of paper bags and always have one eye closed?"

Dunc shook his head again. "These guys look like rejects from the Mafia. Both of them are wearing trench coats and reading newspapers."

Amos rolled his bike forward to get a better look. "Probably drug dealers. We better call it a day and head on home."

"Come on," Dunc said. "We can go down the alley and they probably won't spot us."

"The alley," Amos squeaked. "There are

creepy things in these alleys. Live things. Weirdos. Large man-eating animals. We could get mugged or worse—be eaten alive."

"Get a grip, Amos. Don't let your imagination ruin this. It may be our only chance to get you off the hook with Slasher."

Amos stayed close to Dunc. Closer than his shadow. Which was hard, considering they were on bicycles. Every time he heard a noise, he moved a little closer.

"Move over, Amos. Another couple of inches, and you'll be riding *my* bike."

"Okay. But if something attacks me, I'm holding you personally responsible."

The back door of the abandoned grocery store was locked. The only other entrance was a window about six feet off the ground. It was open about half an inch.

Dunc leaned his bike up against the side of the building. "Give me a boost, Amos. I'm going to try and get through that window. If anybody comes, whistle."

Amos didn't move.

Dunc turned around. "Hurry—we may not have a lot of time."

"We have this little problem, Dunc. I am

40

not staying in this alley alone. There are people—and I use that term loosely—people who would just as soon slit your throat as look at you down here. And there are rodents in these trash cans the size of Volkswagens."

"Amos, you've got to stay here. We can't leave our bikes unguarded. Besides, I need you to keep watch so we don't get caught by Slasher and the gang."

"You always have the right answer for everything, don't you? All right. I'll stay. But it beats me why you would want your best friend in the whole world to be left out here for rat bait."

Chapter · 9

Dunc squeezed through the narrow window. A pile of cardboard boxes broke his fall on the other side. He scrambled to his feet.

"I'm in, Amos. Keep a lookout for anybody suspicious. I won't be long."

Amos backed up against the wall of the building. "There isn't anyone down here who *doesn't* look suspicious."

Dunc adjusted his eyes to the dim light. He looked around the small store. Trash and broken glass covered the floor. An old metal cash register with several missing keys sat on what used to be a checkout

counter. Some of the display shelves still held dusty cans and boxes.

The gang had pulled some wooden crates and a ragged old sofa into a circle. Dunc searched the area carefully. All he found was more trash, an old shoe, and a few broken bottles.

He almost missed it. He walked by it twice. If he hadn't thrown the shoe on the sofa, he might never have seen it.

Wedged in one corner of the sofa, almost hidden from sight, was a folded slip of green paper.

He picked it up carefully and read it.

"Bingo!" yelled Dunc.

Amos was nervously walking up and down the alley behind the store when he heard Dunc yell. He ran over to the window.

"Are you okay in there?"

No answer.

"Dunc."

Amos looked up at the window. He looked around the side of the building. The two Mafia guys were still waiting across the street.

He tried to think. What did Dunc say to do?

Whistle.

Amos started whistling. At first it was a low, raspy whistle. The more excited he got, the louder he got. Finally he worked up to a world-class whistle.

They came out of nowhere.

Dogs.

Big dogs. Little dogs. Mangy, slobbering, *hungry* dogs.

It seemed as if about twenty dogs were coming straight for him. Amos closed his eyes. "This is it. I'm going to die. Dog food in a back alley of the sleaziest part of town . . ."

"Duke. Angel. Stop that."

Amos opened one eye. The dogs were backing off. A scraggly old woman with a shopping cart full of junk was petting the dogs—the whole pack of them. She was scolding them, and they seemed to understand.

She had on two heavy winter coats. Her gray hair was jammed up under a floppy

purple hat. She looked as if she hadn't had a bath in a year. Maybe five.

Amos took a grateful breath. "Are these all your dogs?"

"These ain't nobody's dogs, boy." The old woman smiled. All Amos could see was gums. No teeth. "They's jest like me. They ain't got no home. You can have 'em if you want."

Amos looked at the pack of dogs. "I guess I'd better pass this time. Thanks anyway."

The woman didn't answer. She pushed her cart around the corner. The dogs followed.

"Amos?"

Amos looked up. Dunc was standing on some boxes looking out the window.

"I heard you whistle. Is there a problem?"

"Oh, it's nothing that would concern you. I almost got torn to shreds by a pack of vicious wild animals. No big deal. Don't worry your little head about it."

"Amos, I may be onto something big. Help me down."

Chapter · 10

"Get up, Amos. We're going to be late for school."

"I can't. I'm sick."

"Quit fooling around. We've got work to do."

"I'm too sick. I was fine when I went to bed. But then I started thinking about school and all the ways Slasher could rearrange my body, and I started throwing up. Big chunks. My mom heard me. She said I don't have to go. So I'm not going."

"But Amos, I told you about finding the silver bead and the piece of paper. Don't you

want to put a stop to this guy once and for all?"

Amos sat up. "If you're right—and you rarely are—I have even more reason to stay in this bed."

He plopped back down on the pillows.

"I need your help, Amos. If Slasher and his gang are the stereo thieves, it's our civic duty to put them out of business."

"Why don't you call the cops? This is their line of work, not ours."

Dunc sighed. "I've explained all that to you. We know the silver bead came off of Slasher's jacket. And we know that green slip of paper is a tally sheet for the stereos. But the cops only have our word for it. We've got to get some solid evidence to tie the gang to the crime."

Amos pulled the covers up to his chin. "If you want to play boy detective, go right ahead. But I'm sick. I may be sick for a few days. Weeks. Maybe years. You can never tell about these things."

Dunc waited a few minutes. He hated to do it. But he knew it was the only way. He started walking toward the door.

"Okay, Amos. I understand. No hard feelings. I was sure you'd want the reputation, though. Because of Melissa and all."

Amos moved toward the end of the bed. "Reputation?"

"Sure. When we get through, it'll be all over school how you got the best of Slasher Davis. I mean, it *would* have been all over school."

Amos swung his legs over the side of the bed. "I suppose anybody who got the best of Slasher would be a kind of hero, wouldn't he?"

"I suppose."

"And Melissa would probably hear about it, wouldn't she?"

"Probably."

Amos started to get dressed. "Like I always say, no guts—no glory."

He tied his shoes and hurried past Dunc. "Come on. What are you waiting for?"

"Amos?"

"What? What's the matter?"

"Before you go for the glory, don't you think you'd better put your pants on?"

Chapter · 11

"All things considered, aren't you glad you went to school today?"

Amos snorted. "My head is covered with noogie bumps. My life has been threatened. And you think I should be glad? I should have stayed right here in my room, that's what I should have done."

"Don't let Slasher's little threat worry you."

"Little? He said if I don't have his homework tomorrow, he's going to cut me up in small pieces and flush me. I don't consider that a little threat."

Dunc leaned against the wall. "After we

get through, he won't be around to threaten anybody. You're sure it was tonight?"

"Spit told Crusher they were going shopping in the mall parking lot tonight. Shouldn't we call the cops now?"

"Not just yet. Tonight, after they go for another stereo, we'll follow them. When we find out who the buyer is, then we'll call the police." Dunc looked at his watch. "We'd better get going. We don't know what time they're coming. We need to find a good place to hide."

They made good time getting to the mall. The parking lot was about half full. There would be cars parked there until midnight, when the last movie ended.

They looked around for a hiding place. Everything was out in the open.

Almost everything.

"You call this a good hiding place?" Amos shook his head. "A Dumpster. Have you noticed that we spend a major portion of our time with garbage? Doesn't that seem strange to you?"

Dunc looked over the side. "It's clean.

And you can watch the whole parking lot from here."

"What do you mean, *I* can watch? Where are *you* going to be?"

"I'm going to cruise up and down on my bike. I might be able to spot them when they first pull into the parking lot."

Amos folded his arms. "Why do I have to hide in the garbage while you ride around in the open?"

"If they see you, they might get suspicious. If they see me, they'll think I'm just another kid on the way to the mall."

Amos climbed into the Dumpster. "Somehow I knew you'd have it covered."

Dunc pulled away. "Whistle—I mean, call if you need me."

The Dumpster was fairly empty. A few boxes and plastic bags were piled in one corner. Amos stood in another corner and watched the parking lot.

He watched cars and people until he thought his eyes would pop out. He had been watching for over two hours, and the gang still hadn't shown up.

The door of the Dumpster rattled. Some-one was opening it. Amos crouched in the corner. A man wearing a white apron tossed in some pizza boxes. He barely missed Amos. Then he threw in a big plastic sack full of old spaghetti and salad.

This time he didn't miss.

Amos pulled a lettuce leaf off his head. Some of the spaghetti stuck in his hair.

"This is it. I've had enough."

He started climbing out when Dunc rode up.

"What happened to you?"

"Don't ask."

Dunc helped him down. "I've spotted them. Slasher is in that blue car on the fifth row. Get ready."

They watched the gang spread out to look for security guards. Slasher was fast. He was in and out in three minutes. The gang met him by the stop sign with his bike. They took off down the street.

Dunc started after them. "Come on, Amos."

They followed at a distance. The first

stop was a pawnshop called Fast Eddie's. Slasher was only inside for a few minutes. Apparently Fast Eddie didn't need any stolen car stereos today. Slasher stuffed it under his jacket and rode off.

The gang took off again. This time they headed for the waterfront. They rode straight to the old store without stopping. Slasher kicked the door open and walked in.

Dunc pulled over a few blocks from the store. "We'll go around back. It might be possible for us to hear something from the window."

"Haven't we got enough to call the police? We could go on home and let them take care of it from here," Amos argued.

Dunc chewed his lip. "We could do that. But we're already here. It won't hurt to listen. Just a couple of minutes, then we're gone. I promise."

They hid their bikes in the bushes and quietly inched up to the window. Amos boosted Dunc up.

He could see the gang sitting in the circle. They were discussing their next move.

Apparently Fast Eddie bought from them once in a while, but most of the time it was another man—an important business-man who sold car stereos and electronics in a fancy store uptown.

Dunc memorized the information. He was ready to go. He started to step down.

An alley cat had been eyeing Amos. She could smell the spaghetti on his clothes. First she rubbed up against his leg. Then she jumped up onto his shoulder and licked his face.

Amos let go of Dunc, which left him hanging from the window ledge. The cat started yowling and dug her claws into Amos's back. He was turning circles trying to reach her.

Someone jerked the cat off.

"Look what we have here, boys! A couple of peeping geeks."

Slasher pushed Amos toward the door. "Get the Brain!" he barked over his shoulder.

Dunc dropped to the ground and followed Amos inside the building.

Slasher took out his switchblade and

clicked it open. He pointed it at the couch. "Have a seat, geeks."

Amos looked at Dunc.

Slasher pointed the knife at Amos. "What are you doing down here, Barf Bag?"

"That's Dirt Bag," Amos corrected. "Would you believe we were out for a late-night bike ride, and of all places we ended up here?"

Spit, the short one with his name shaved in his hair, stepped over. "Like, that's a major coincidence, man."

Slasher shook his head. "Shut up, stupid. Anybody with half a brain can see they're down here spying on us."

Amos leaned over and whispered in Dunc's ear, "That leaves him out."

Spit's shoulders drooped. He put his head down and stepped back.

Slasher started cleaning his fingernails with the switchblade. "We can't have you geeks talking to the cops now, can we? What are we gonna do with you? Anybody got any ideas?"

The front door flew open.

"We may have a few."

It was the two Mafia guys from across the street. "You punks get up against the wall and spread 'em. You have the right to remain silent. . . ."

Chapter · 12

Dunc was reading the newspaper in his room. " 'Car stereo burglars nabbed by police. Ring busted wide open. Prominent businessman in custody.' "

"It figures they wouldn't mention us," Amos said.

"I guess they already had Slasher and his gang under surveillance. They probably thought we were just in the way."

Amos picked up the newspaper. "They wouldn't have gotten the main buyer if it hadn't been for us."

59

"That's true. But if those two undercover cops hadn't been there last night, we might have been in serious trouble. And there is one other consolation."

Amos yawned. "What's that?"

"Slasher won't be bothering you anymore."

"That part's good. But I was hoping Melissa would hear about it and fall at my feet in hero worship. Then we'd get married sometime next week and live happily ever after."

"I'm sorry things didn't work out for you, Amos."

"Oh, well. At least this whole thing hasn't been a total loss."

Dunc looked surprised. "Why, Amos. I'm proud of you. I thought you'd really be upset about not getting your name in the paper and all. I think you're taking a very mature outlook on this."

Amos put his hands behind his head. "Yeah, that's me. I'm a mature sort of guy. Besides, I still have Amy's diary. She's promised to do all my chores for the next

year if I'll give it back. I'm still thinking about it. I think I'll let her beg and grovel at my feet for a while."

Dunc grinned. "A real mature guy . . ."

Be sure to join Dunc and Amos in these other Culpepper Adventures:

The Case of the Dirty Bird

When Dunc Culpepper and his best friend, Amos, first see the parrot in a pet store, they're not impressed—it's smelly, scruffy, and missing half its feathers. They're only slightly impressed when they learn that the parrot speaks four languages, has outlived ten of its owners, and is probably 150 years old. But when the bird starts mouthing off about buried treasure, Dunc and Amos get pretty excited—let the amateur sleuthing begin!

Dunc's Doll

Dunc and his accident-prone friend Amos are up to their old sleuthing habits once again. This time they're after a band of doll thieves! When a doll that once belonged to Charles Dickens's daughter is stolen from an exhibition at the local mall, the two boys put on their detective gear and do some serious snooping. Will a vi-

cious watchdog keep them from retrieving the valuable missing doll?

Culpepper's Cannon

Dunc and Amos are researching the Civil War cannon that stands in the town square when they find a note inside telling them about a time portal. Entering it through the dressing room of La Petite, a women's clothing store, the boys find themselves in downtown Chatham on March 8, 1862—the day before the historic clash between the *Monitor* and the *Merrimac*. But the Confederate soldiers they meet mistake them for Yankee spies. Will they make it back to the future in one piece?

Dunc Gets Tweaked

Dunc and Amos meet up with a new buddy named Lash when they enter the radical world of skateboard competition. When somebody "cops"—steals—Lash's prototype skateboard, the boys are determined to get it back. After all, Lash is about to shoot for a totally rad world's record! Along the way they learn a major lesson: *Never* kiss a monkey!

Dunc's Halloween

Dunc and Amos are planning the best route to get the most candy on Halloween. But their plans change when Amos is slightly bitten by a werewolf. He begins scratching himself and chasing UPS trucks—he's become a werepuppy!

Dunc Breaks the Record

Dunc and Amos have a small problem when they try hang gliding—they crash in the wilderness. Luckily, Amos has read a book about a boy who survived in the wilderness for fifty-four days. Too bad Amos doesn't have a hatchet. Things go from bad to worse when a wild man holds the boys captive. Can anything save them now?

Dunc and the Flaming Ghost

Dunc's not afraid of ghosts, although Amos is sure that the old Rambridge house is haunted by the ghost of Blackbeard the Pirate. Then the best friends meet Eddie, a meek man who claims to be impersonating Blackbeard's ghost in order to live in the house in peace. But if that's true, why are flames shooting from his mouth?

Amos Gets Famous

Deciphering a code they find in a library book, Amos and Dunc stumble onto a burglary ring. The burglars' next target is the home of Melissa, the girl of Amos's dreams (who doesn't even know that he's alive). Amos longs to be a hero to Melissa, so nothing will stop him from solving this case—not even a mind-boggling collision with a jock, a chimpanzee, and a toilet.

Dunc and Amos Hit the Big Top

In order to impress Melissa, Amos decides to perform on the trapeze at the visiting circus. Look out below! But before Dunc can talk him out of his plan, the two stumble across a mystery behind the scenes at the circus. Now Amos is in double trouble. What's really going on under the big top?

Dunc's Dump

Camouflaged as piles of rotting trash, Dunc and Amos are sneaking around the town dump. Dunc wants to find out who is polluting the garbage at the dump with hazardous and toxic waste. Amos just wants to impress Melissa. Can either of them succeed?

Dunc and the Scam Artists

Dunc and Amos are at it again. Some older residents of their town have been bilked by con artists, and the two boys want to look into these crimes. They meet elderly Betsy Dell, whose nasty nephew Frank gives the boys the creeps. Then they notice some soft dirt in Ms. Dell's shed, and a shovel. Does Frank have something horrible in store for Dunc and Amos?

Dunc and Amos and the Red Tattoos

Dunc and Amos head for camp and face two weeks of fresh air—along with regulations, demerits, KP, and inedible food. But where these two best friends go, trouble follows. They overhear a threat against the camp director, and discover that camp funds have been stolen. Do these crimes have anything to do with the tattoo of the exotic red flower that some of the camp staff have on their arms?

Dunc's Undercover Christmas

It's Christmastime! and Dunc, Amos, and Amos's cousin T.J. hit the mall for some serious shopping. But when the seasonal magic is threatened by some disappearing presents, and Santa Claus himself is a prime suspect, the

boys put their celebration on hold and go undercover in perfect Christmas disguises! Can the sleuthing trio protect Santa's threatened reputation and catch the impostor before he strikes again?

The Wild Culpepper Cruise

When Amos wins a "Why I Love My Dog" contest, he and Dunc are off on the Caribbean cruise of their dreams! But there's something downright fishy about Amos's suitcase, and before they know it, the two best friends wind up with more high-seas adventure than they bargained for. Can Dunc and Amos figure out who's out to get them and salvage what's left of their vacation?

Dunc and the Haunted Castle

When Dunc and Amos are invited to spend a week in Scotland, Dunc can already hear the bagpipes a-blowin'. But when the boys spend their first night in an ancient castle, it isn't bagpipes they hear. It's moans! Dunc hears groaning coming from inside his bedroom walls. Amos notices the eyes of a painting follow him across the room! Could the castle really be haunted? Local legend has it that the castle's

former lord wanders the ramparts at night in search of his head! Team up with Dunc and Amos as they go ghostbusting in the Scottish Highlands!

Cowpokes and Desperadoes

Git along, little dogies! Dunc and Amos are bound for Uncle Woody Culpepper's Santa Fe cattle ranch for a week of fun. But when they overhear a couple of cowpokes plotting to do Uncle Woody in, the two sleuths are back on the trail of some serious action! Who's been making off with all the prize cattle? Can Dunc and Amos stop the rustlers in time to save the ranch?

Prince Amos

When their fifth-grade class spends a weekend interning at the state capital, Dunc and Amos find themselves face-to-face with Amos's walking double—Prince Gustav, Crown Prince of Moldavia! His Royal Highness is desperate to uncover a traitor in his ranks. And when he asks Amos to switch places with him, Dunc holds his breath to see what will happen next. Can Amos pull off the impersonation of a lifetime?

Coach Amos

Amos and Dunc have their hands full when their school principal asks *them* to coach a local T-ball team. For one thing, nobody on the team even knows first base from left field, and the season opener is coming right up. And then there's that sinister-looking gangster driving by in his long black limo and making threats. Can Dunc and Amos fend off screaming tots, nervous mothers, and the mob, and be there when the ump yells "Play ball"?

Amos and the Alien

When Amos and his best friend Dunc have a close encounter with an extraterrestrial named Girrk, Dunc thinks they should report their findings to NASA. But Amos has other plans. He not only promises to help Girrk find a way back to his planet, he invites him to hide out under his bed! Then weird things start to happen—Scruff can't move, Amos scores a game-winning *touchdown,* and Dunc knows Girrk is behind Amos's new powers. What's the mysterious alien really up to?